04120451

1133087

D0541536

TOKYNGTON LIBRARY
Monks Park
Wembley HA9 6JE
020 8937 3590
This book is due for return on or before the last date shown below

1 8 APR 2006

23 ....

1 0 FEB 2007

1 0 MAR 2007

1 - MAY 2007

0 5 JUN 2007   0 3 SEP 2005

0 1 OCT 2007   1 0 SEP 2005

2 7 NOV 2007

0 4 FEB 2008   2 0 MAY 2006
                     1 3 NOV 200

FRIENDS
by Kathryn Cave and Nick Maland
British Library Cataloguing in Publication Data
A catalogue record of this book is
available from the British Library.

ISBN 0 340 71608 8 (HB)
ISBN 0 340 65600 X (PB)

Text copyright © Kathryn Cave 2004
Illustrations copyright © Nick Maland 2004

The right of Kathryn Cave to be identified as
the author and Nick Maland as the illustrator of
this Work has been asserted by them in accordance
with the Copyright, Designs and Patents Act 1988.

First HB edition published 2004
This PB edition published 2005
10 9 8 7 6 5 4 3 2 1

Published by Hodder Children's Books
a division of Hodder Headline Limited
338 Euston Road London NW1 3BH

Printed in China
All rights reserved

The illustrations in this book were made
with watercolour on photocopied drawings.

BRENT LIBRARY
SERVICE

6 MAY 2005   £5·99

BfS   TOK

04120451

For my dear friends, past, present and future. **K.C.**

For my friends, Mark and Johnny. **N.M.**

Friends

Written by **Kathryn Cave**

Illustrated by **Nick Maland**

*Hodder
Children's
Books*

A division of Hodder Headline Limited

Once I was lost
in the wood,
in the wood,

and you
found me.

Once I fell down.
I hurt my knee.
You put your arms around me.

Once I was shy,
I didn't know where to go,
until you saw me.

Once I was slow,
I couldn't catch up.
You waited for me.

Once I was afraid
of the dark, of the dark,
and the creatures that
hide there.

You didn't laugh
and it wasn't so bad,
with you at my side there.

Once I got cross.
I really yelled.
You got cross, too.

When I stopped being cross,
I felt sad and alone.
I thought I'd lost you.

But I hadn't.

'Want to be friends?'

'OK.'

If you are lost
in the wood, in the wood,
I will find you.

If you're afraid
of the cold and the dark,
I'll sit beside you.

I'll wait for you,
I'll share with you,
I'll comfort you,
I'll care for you
the way you cared for me.

That's what friends do.

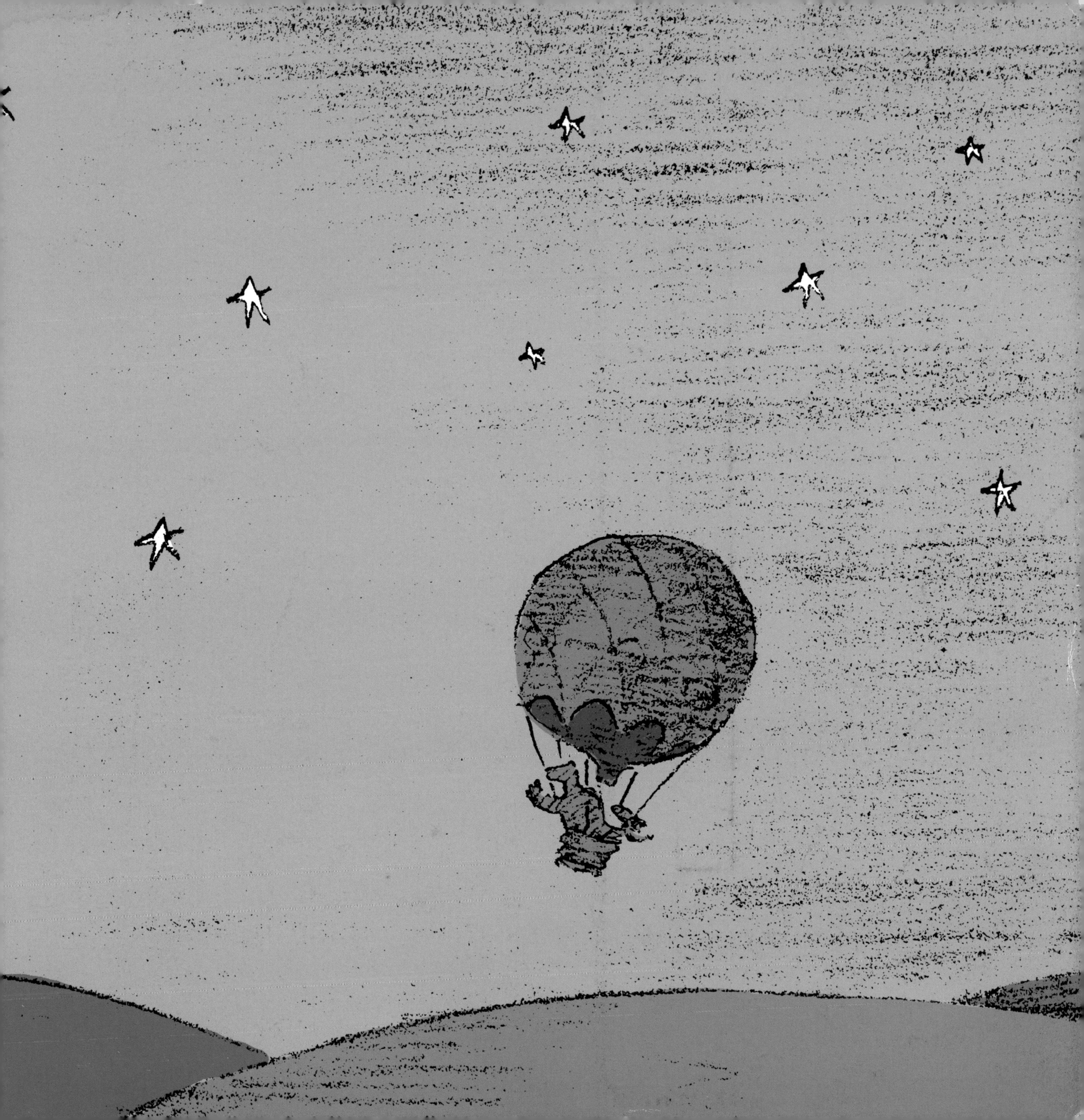